REBEL JAIL: VOLUME 2

It is an era of renewed hope for the Rebellion.

After narrowly escaping another frightening encounter with Darth Vader, rebel heroes Luke Skywalker, Princess Leia, and Han Solo take the evil Sith Lord's secret ally, droid and weapon specialist Dr. Aphra, captive aboard the Millennium Falcon.

Now their mission to free the galaxy from the grasp of the Emperor continues as the Princess teams with smuggler Sana Starros, while Luke and Han pair together on a secret mission for the Rebellion....

JASON AARON
Writer

LEINIL FRANCIS YU
Penciler

GERRY ALANGUILAN
Inker

SUNNY GHO
Colorist

CHRIS ELIOPOULOS
Letterer

TERRY DODSON & RACHEL DODSON
Cover Artists

HEATHER ANTOS
Assistant Editor

JORDAN D. WHITE
Editor

C.B. CEBULSKI
Executive Editor

AXEL ALONSO
Editor In Chief

JOE QUESADA
Chief Creative Officer

DAN BUCKLEY
Publisher

For Lucasfilm:
Creative Director MICHAEL SIGLAIN
Senior Editor FRANK PARISI
Lucasfilm Story Group RAYNE ROBERTS, PABLO HIDALGO, LELAND CHEE

ABDO
Spotlight

ABDOPUBLISHING.COM

Reinforced library bound edition published in 2018 by Spotlight,
a division of ABDO, PO Box 398166, Minneapolis, Minnesota 55439.
Spotlight produces high-quality reinforced library bound editions for
schools and libraries. Published by agreement with Marvel Characters, Inc.

Printed in the United States of America, North Mankato, Minnesota.
092017
012018

marvelkids.com

PUBLISHER'S CATALOGING-IN-PUBLICATION DATA

Names: Aaron, Jason, author. I Mayhew, Mike; Yu, Leinil Francis; Alanguilan, Gerry;
    Gho, Sunny; Tartaglia, Java, illustrators.
Title: Rebel jail / writer: Jason Aaron ; art: Mike Mayhew; Leinil Francis Yu; Gerry
    Alanguilan; Sunny Gho; Java Tartaglia.
Description: Reinforced library bound edition. I Minneapolis, MN : Spotlight, 2018 I
    Series: Star Wars: Rebel jail I Volume 1 written by Jason Aaron ; illustrated by
    Mike Mayhew. I Volumes 2 and 4 written by Jason Aaron ; illustrated by Leinil
    Francis Yu; Gerry Alanguilan & Sunny Gho. I Volume 3 written by Jason Aaron ;
    illustrated by Leinil Francis Yu & Sunny Gho. I Volume 5 written by Jason Aaron ;
    illustrated by Leinil Francis Yu; Gerry Alanguilan; Sunny Gho & Java Tartaglia.
Summary: During Ben Kenobi's exile on Tatooine, he vows to keep a young Luke
    safe; Princess Leia and Sana Starros bring an important captive to the Sunspot
    Prison, where they are ambushed by a rebel spy on a mission of life and death;
    Luke Skywalker tries his hand at smuggling after Han loses their rebel funds in a
    gamble.
Identifiers: LCCN 2017941922 I ISBN 9781532141416 (volume 1) I ISBN
    9781532141423 (volume 2) I ISBN 9781532141430 (volume 3) I ISBN
    9781532141447 (volume 4) I ISBN 9781532141454 (volume 5)
Subjects: LCSH: Star Wars (film)--Juvenile fiction. I Adventure and Adventurers--
    Juvenile fiction. I Graphic Novels--Juvenile fiction.
Classification: DDC 741.5--dc23
LC record available at http://lccn.loc.gov/2017941922

Spotlight

A Division of ABDO
abdopublishing.com

STAR WARS

™

REBEL JAIL

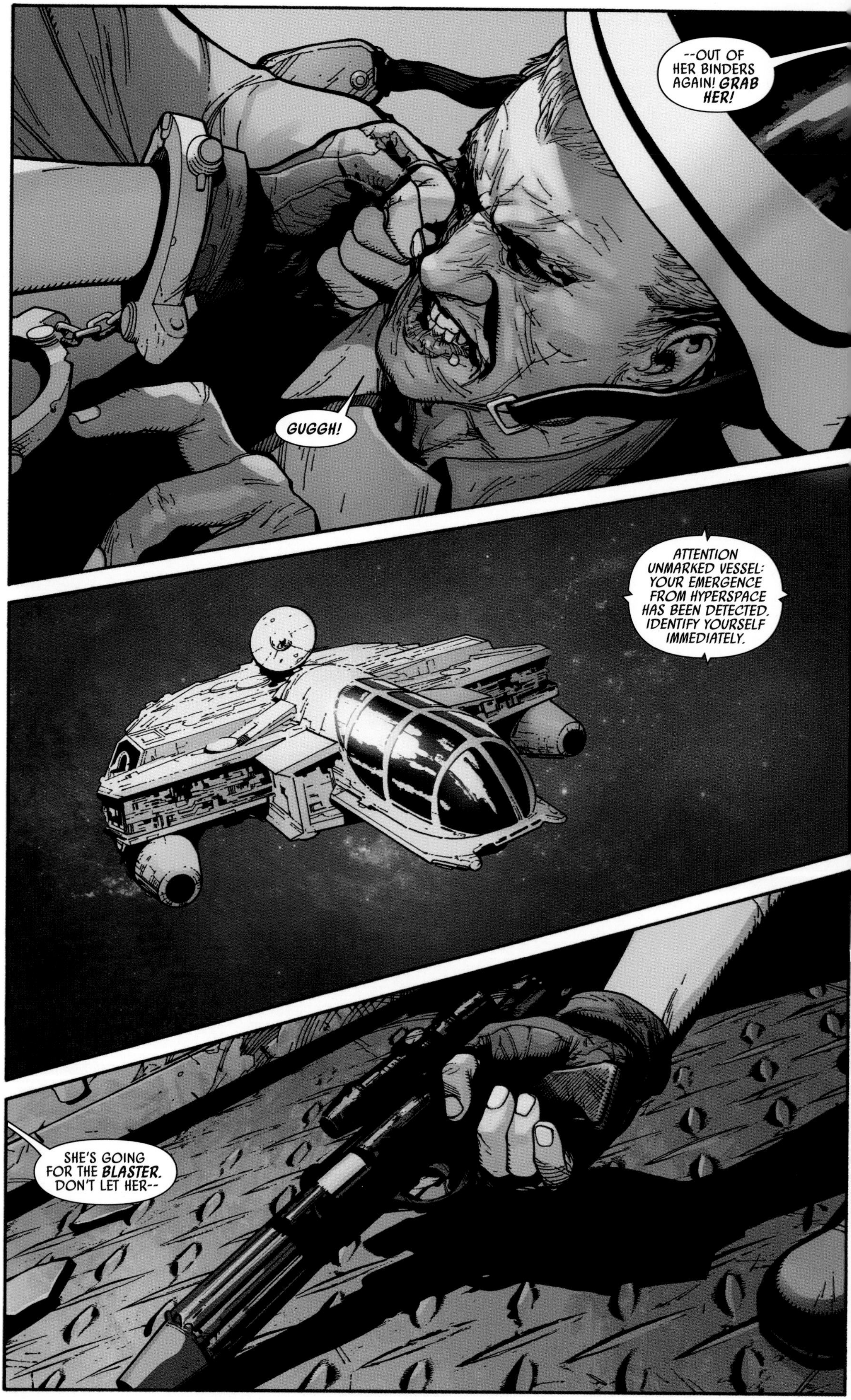
--OUT OF HER BINDERS AGAIN! GRAB HER!
GUGGH!
ATTENTION UNMARKED VESSEL: YOUR EMERGENCE FROM HYPERSPACE HAS BEEN DETECTED. IDENTIFY YOURSELF IMMEDIATELY.
SHE'S GOING FOR THE BLASTER. DON'T LET HER--

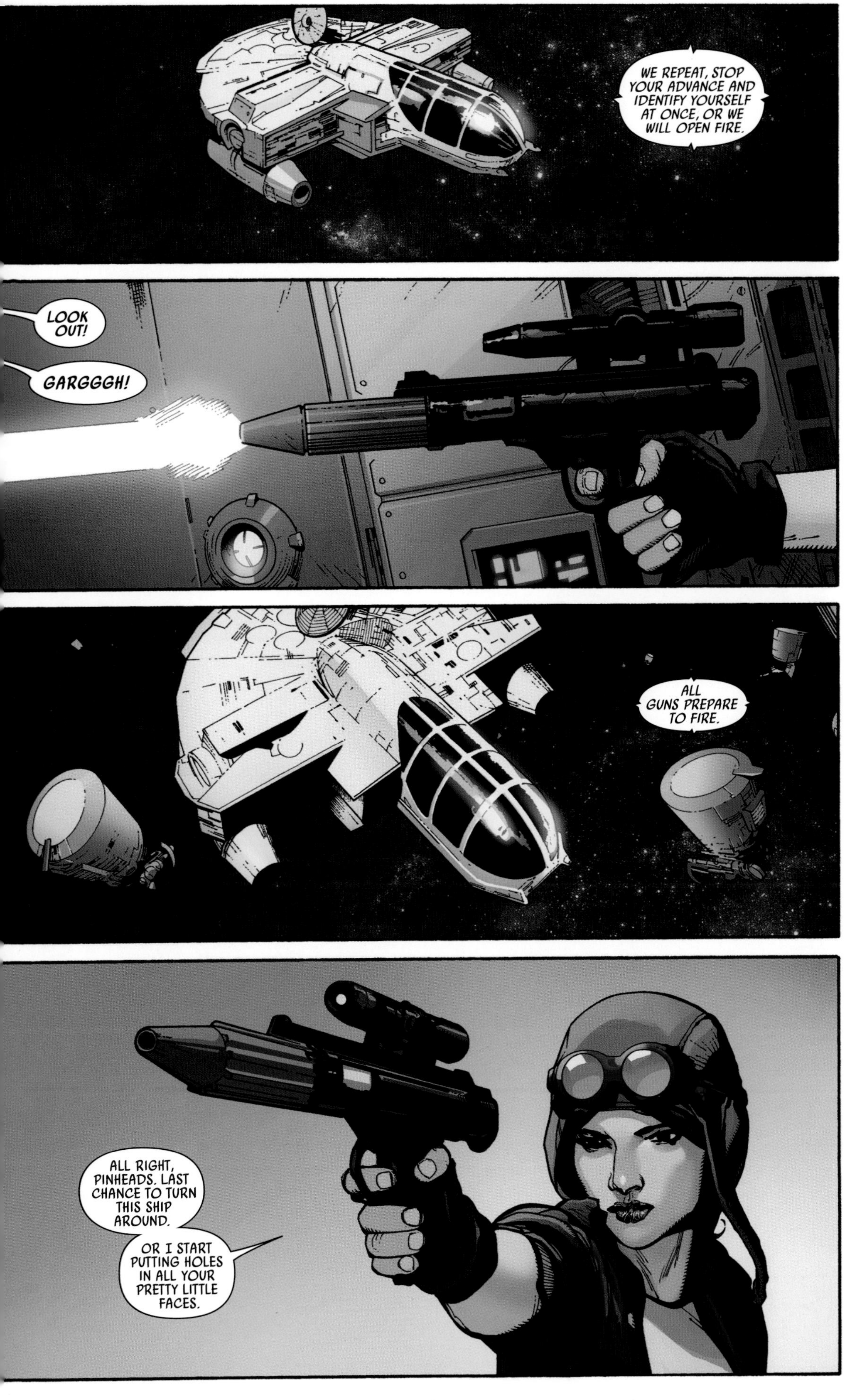
WE REPEAT, STOP YOUR ADVANCE AND IDENTIFY YOURSELF AT ONCE, OR WE WILL OPEN FIRE.
LOOK OUT!
GARGGGH!
ALL GUNS PREPARE TO FIRE.
ALL RIGHT, PINHEADS. LAST CHANCE TO TURN THIS SHIP AROUND.
OR I START PUTTING HOLES IN ALL YOUR PRETTY LITTLE FACES.

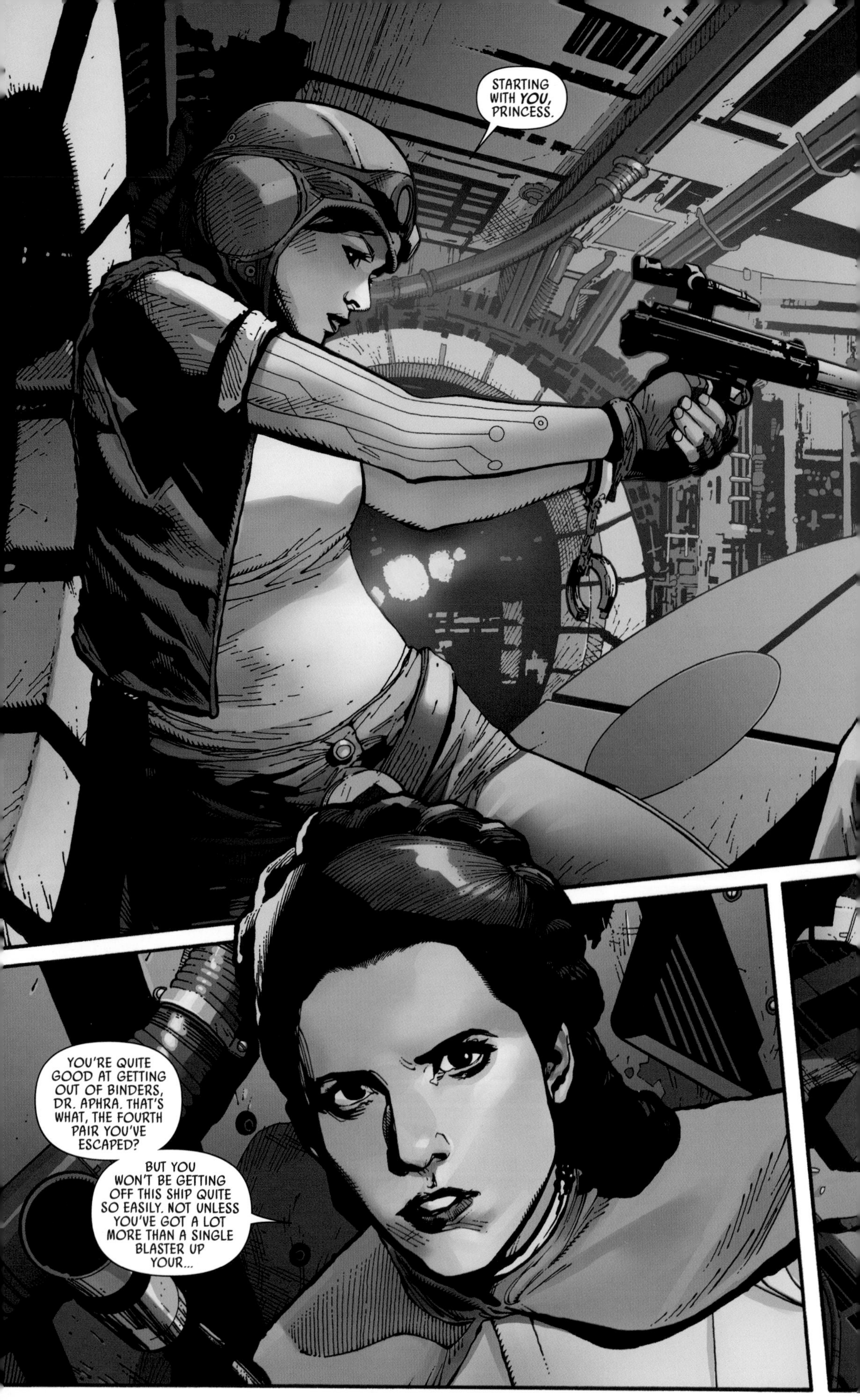
STARTING WITH *YOU*, PRINCESS.
YOU'RE QUITE GOOD AT GETTING OUT OF BINDERS, DR. APHRA. THAT'S WHAT, THE FOURTH PAIR YOU'VE ESCAPED?
BUT YOU WON'T BE GETTING OFF THIS SHIP QUITE SO EASILY. NOT UNLESS YOU'VE GOT A LOT MORE THAN A SINGLE BLASTER UP YOUR...

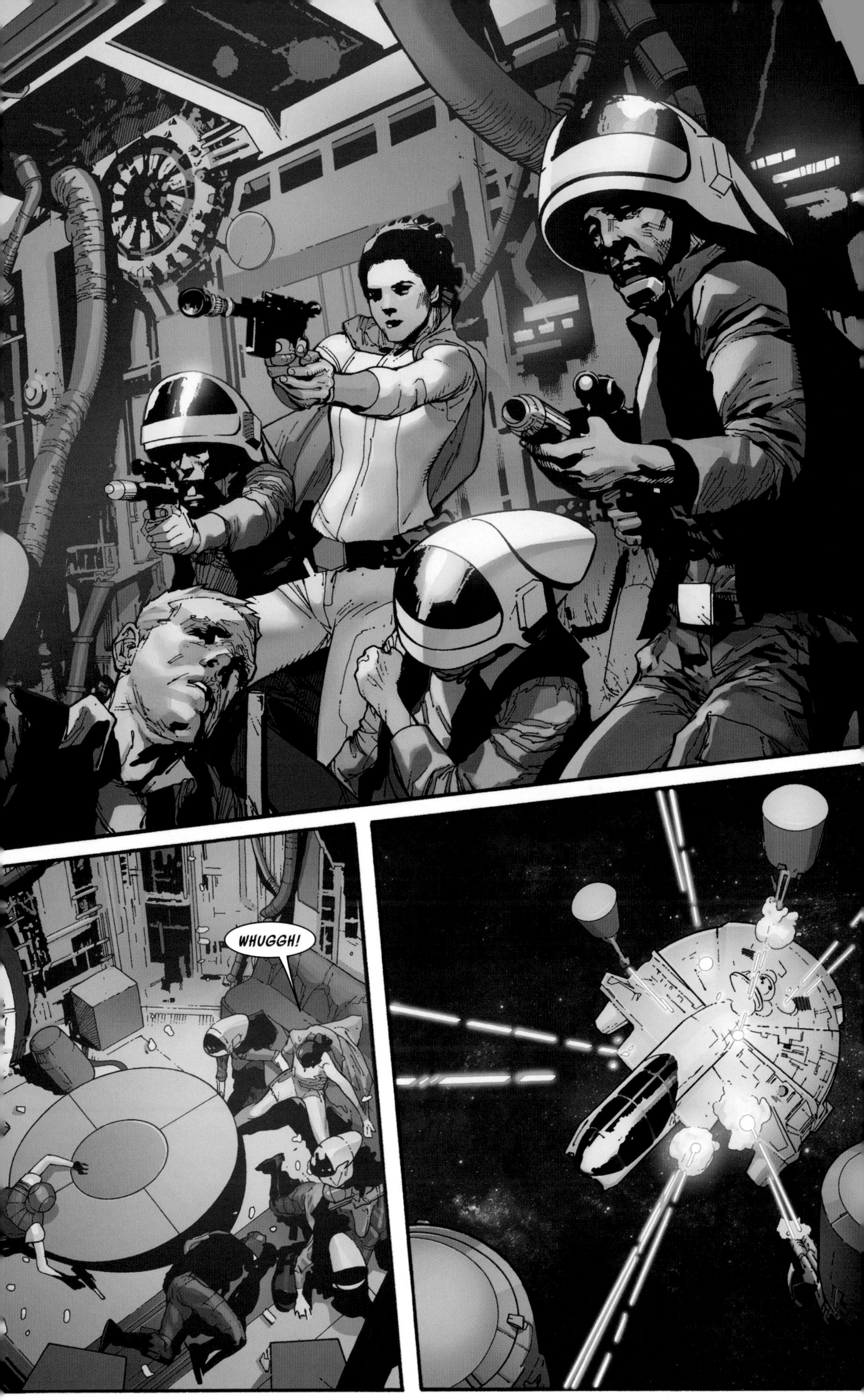
WHUGGH!

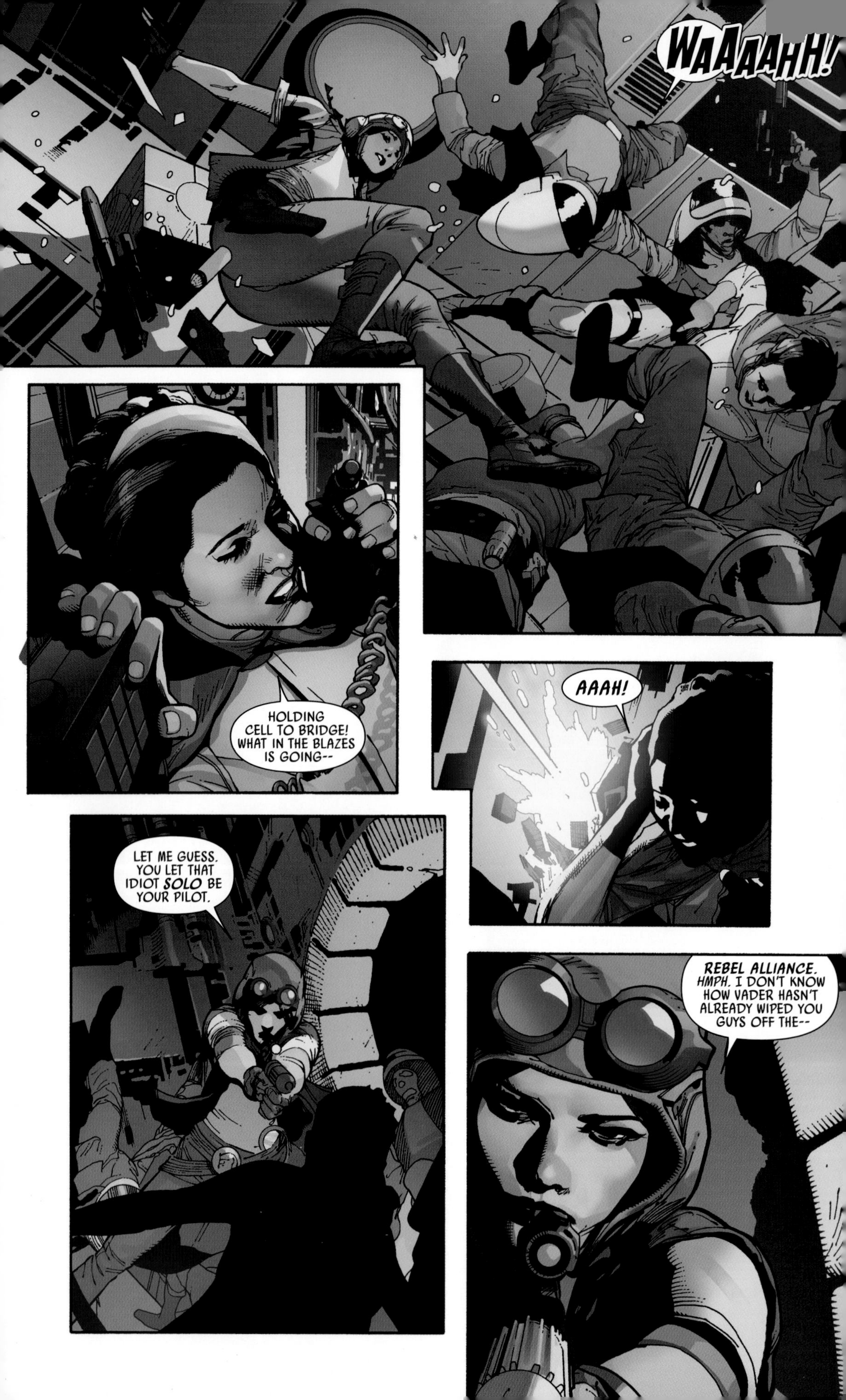
WAAAAHH!
HOLDING CELL TO BRIDGE! WHAT IN THE BLAZES IS GOING--
AAAH!
LET ME GUESS. YOU LET THAT IDIOT SOLO BE YOUR PILOT.
REBEL ALLIANCE. HMPH. I DON'T KNOW HOW VADER HASN'T ALREADY WIPED YOU GUYS OFF THE--

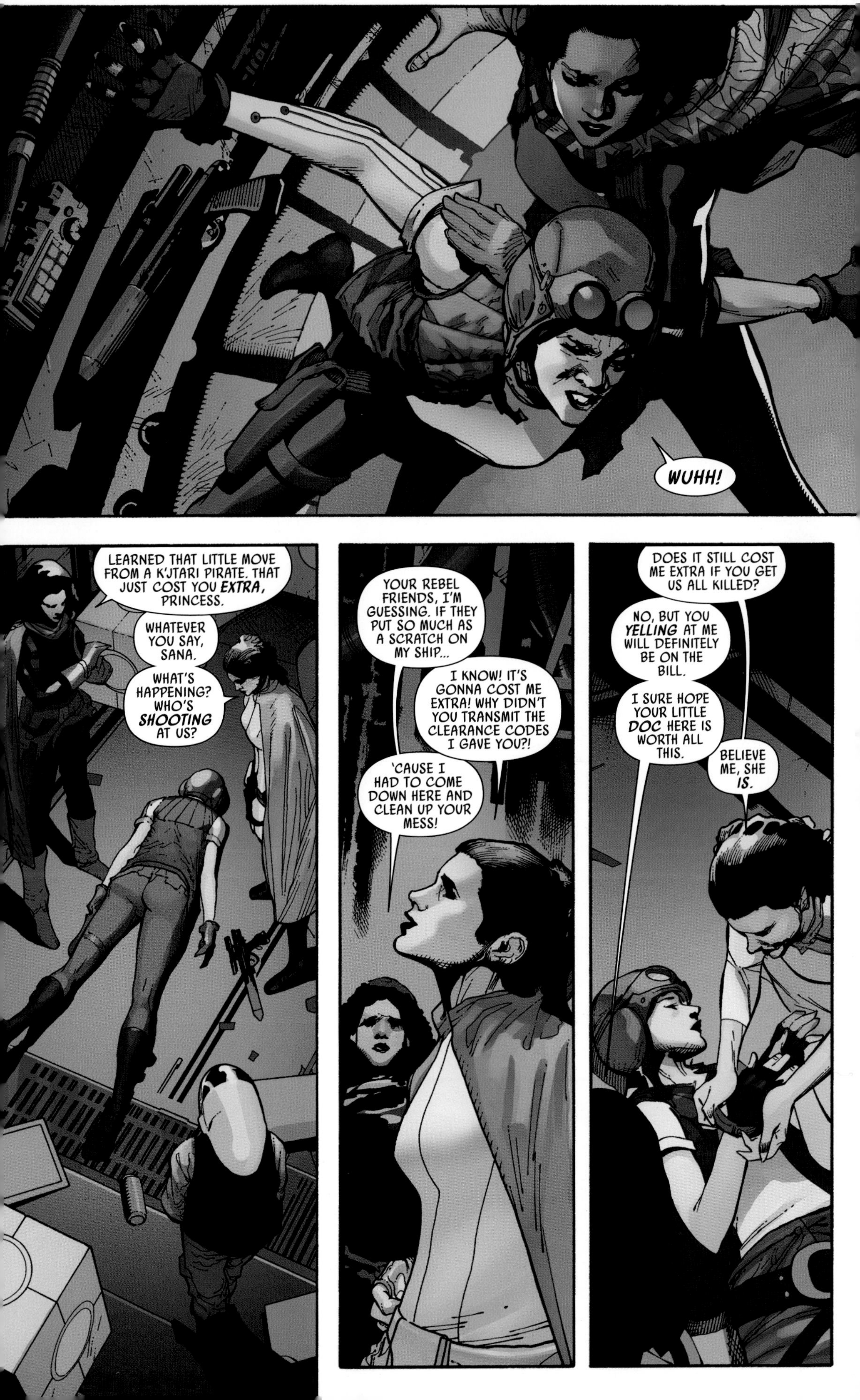
WUHH!
LEARNED THAT LITTLE MOVE FROM A K'JTARI PIRATE. THAT JUST COST YOU EXTRA, PRINCESS.
WHATEVER YOU SAY, SANA.
WHAT'S HAPPENING? WHO'S SHOOTING AT US?
YOUR REBEL FRIENDS, I'M GUESSING. IF THEY PUT SO MUCH AS A SCRATCH ON MY SHIP...
I KNOW! IT'S GONNA COST ME EXTRA! WHY DIDN'T YOU TRANSMIT THE CLEARANCE CODES I GAVE YOU?!
'CAUSE I HAD TO COME DOWN HERE AND CLEAN UP YOUR MESS!
DOES IT STILL COST ME EXTRA IF YOU GET US ALL KILLED?
NO, BUT YOU YELLING AT ME WILL DEFINITELY BE ON THE BILL.
I SURE HOPE YOUR LITTLE DOC HERE IS WORTH ALL THIS.
BELIEVE ME, SHE IS.

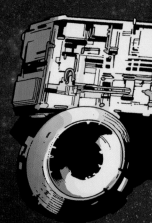

CODES CLEARED. YOU MAY PROCEED.

SORRY IF WE ROUGHED YOU UP A LITTLE, **VOLT COBRA**. CAN'T AFFORD TO BE TOO CAREFUL AT A FACILITY LIKE THIS.

WELCOME TO A PLACE THAT DOESN'T OFFICIALLY EXIST.

THE BIGGEST, BADDEST PENITENTIARY THE ALLIANCE HAS TO OFFER.

MAY YOUR STAY HERE BE A **SHORT** ONE.

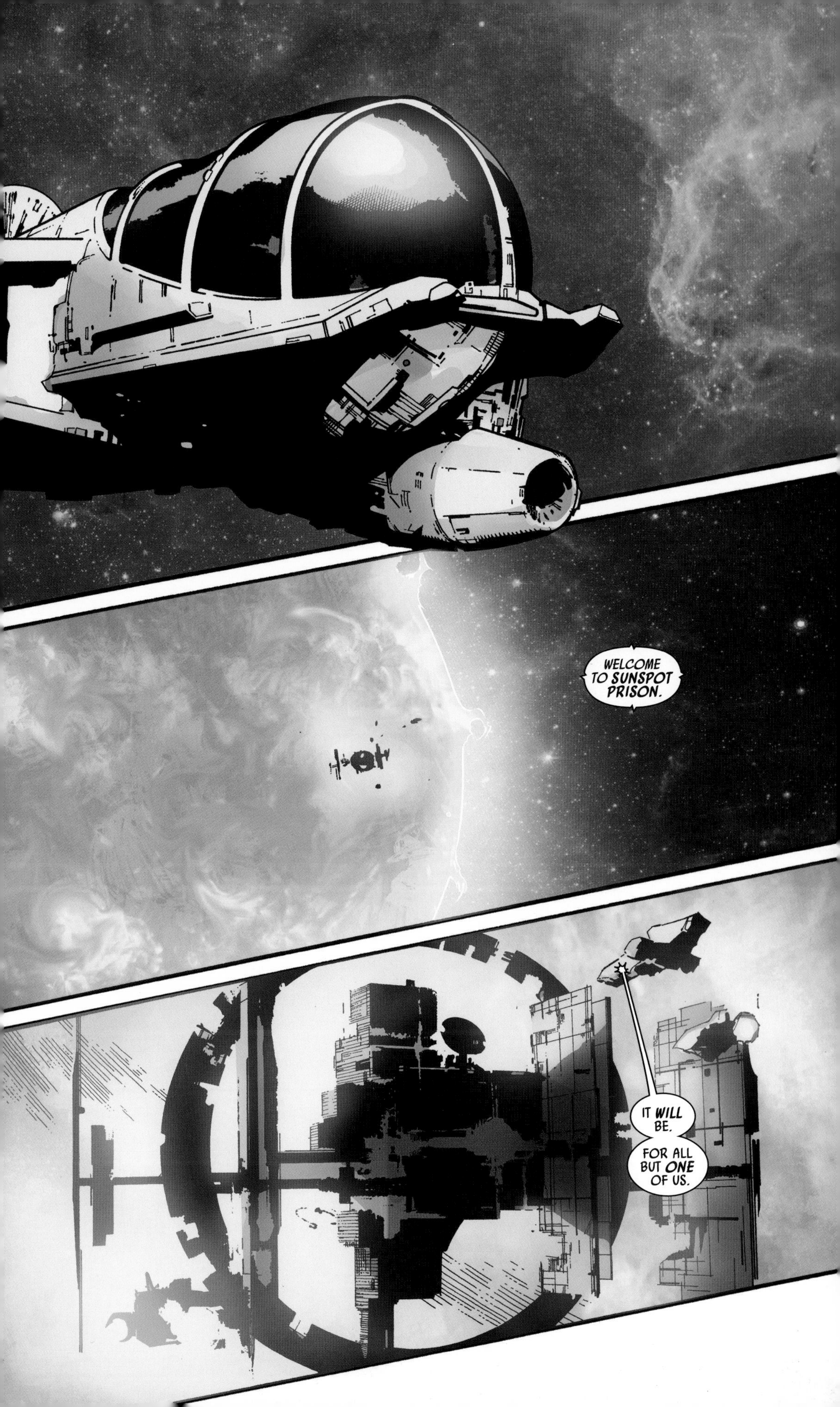
WELCOME TO SUNSPOT PRISON.
IT WILL BE.
FOR ALL BUT ONE OF US.

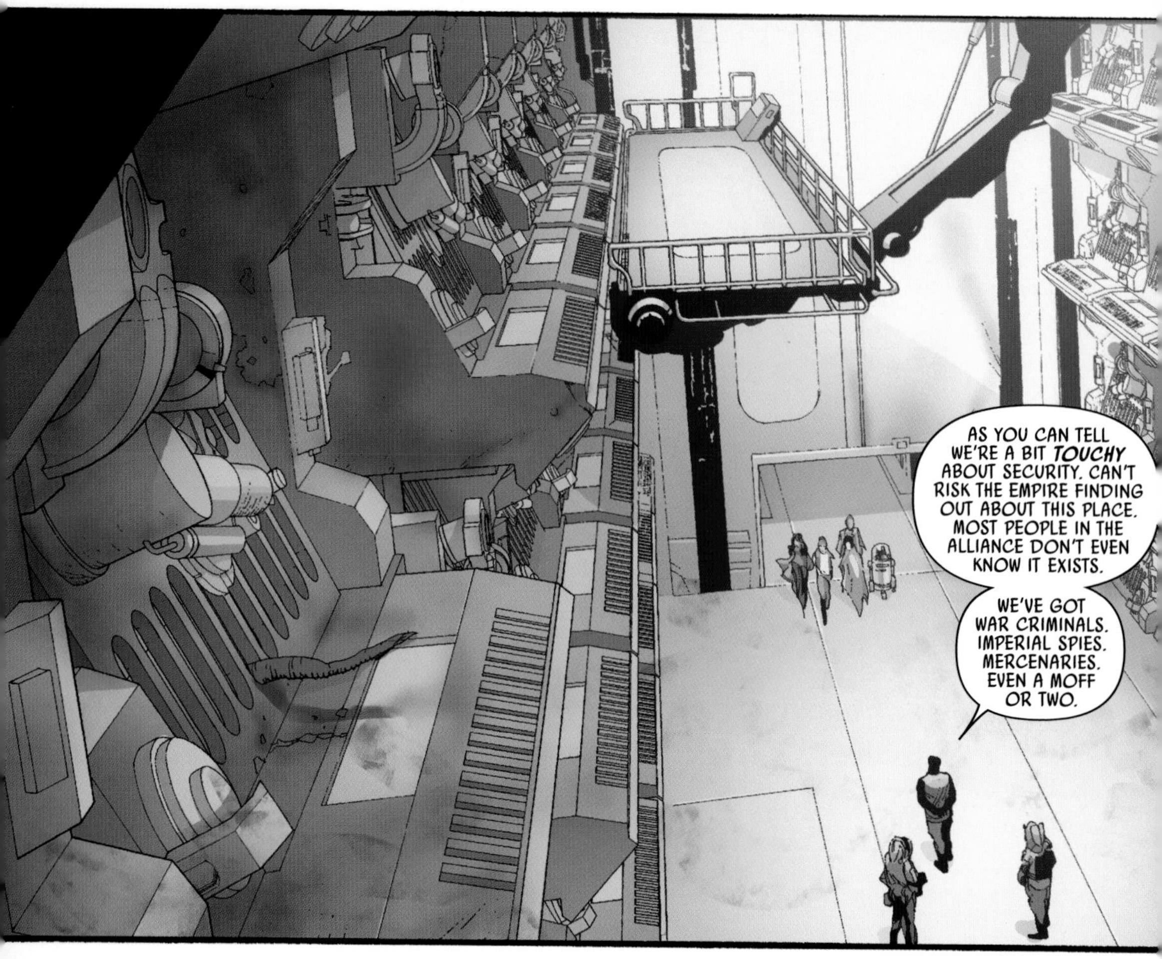
AS YOU CAN TELL WE'RE A BIT *TOUCHY* ABOUT SECURITY. CAN'T RISK THE EMPIRE FINDING OUT ABOUT THIS PLACE. MOST PEOPLE IN THE ALLIANCE DON'T EVEN KNOW IT EXISTS.
WE'VE GOT WAR CRIMINALS. IMPERIAL SPIES. MERCENARIES. EVEN A MOFF OR TWO.

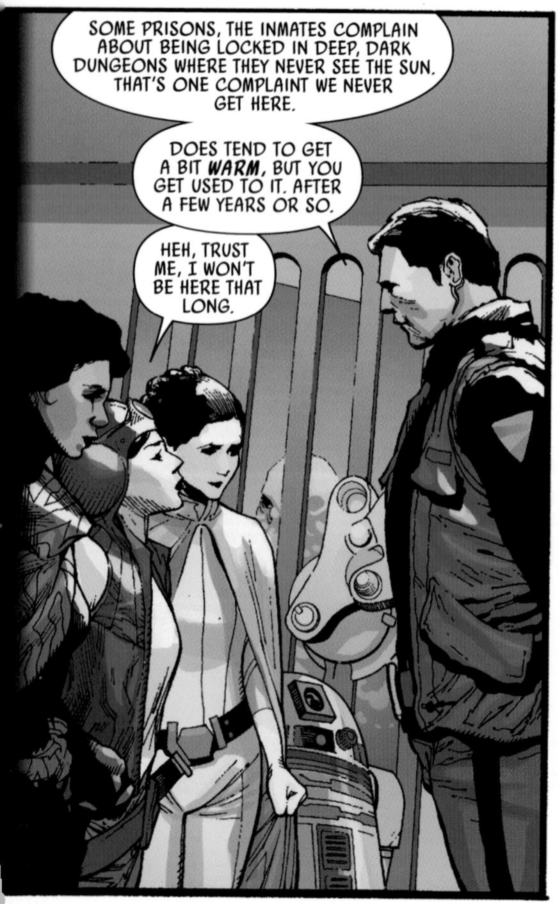
SOME PRISONS, THE INMATES COMPLAIN ABOUT BEING LOCKED IN DEEP, DARK DUNGEONS WHERE THEY NEVER SEE THE SUN. THAT'S ONE COMPLAINT WE NEVER GET HERE.
DOES TEND TO GET A BIT ***WARM,*** BUT YOU GET USED TO IT. AFTER A FEW YEARS OR SO.
HEH, TRUST ME, I WON'T BE HERE THAT LONG.

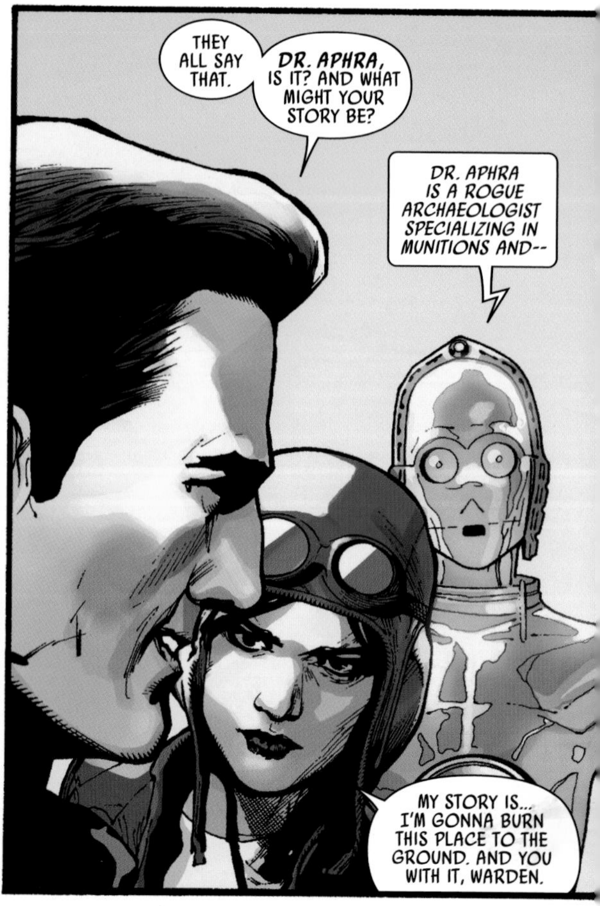
THEY ALL SAY THAT.
DR. APHRA, IS IT? AND WHAT MIGHT YOUR STORY BE?
DR. APHRA IS A ROGUE ARCHAEOLOGIST SPECIALIZING IN MUNITIONS AND--
MY STORY IS... I'M GONNA BURN THIS PLACE TO THE GROUND. AND YOU WITH IT, WARDEN.

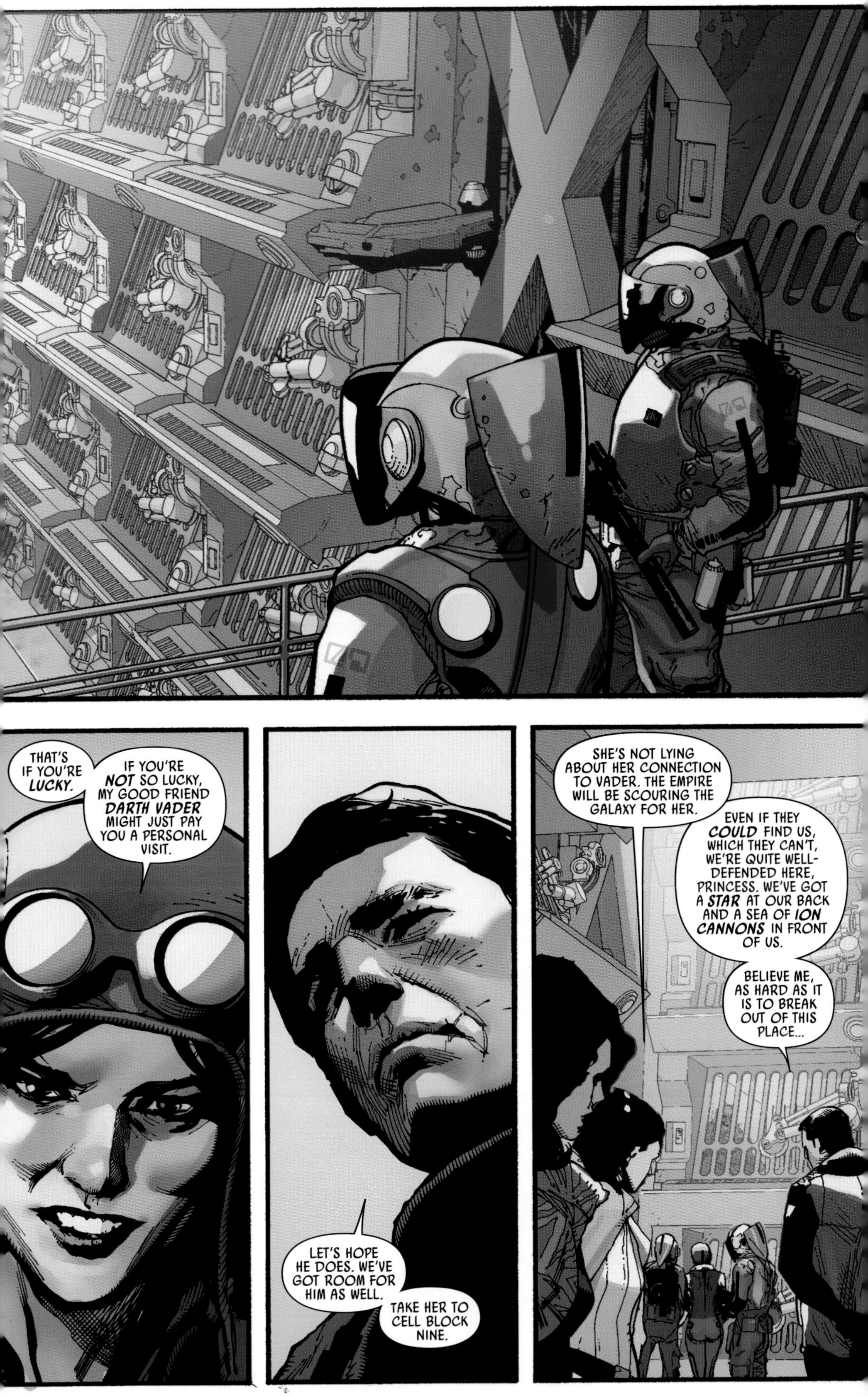

THAT'S IF YOU'RE LUCKY.
IF YOU'RE NOT SO LUCKY, MY GOOD FRIEND DARTH VADER MIGHT JUST PAY YOU A PERSONAL VISIT.
LET'S HOPE HE DOES. WE'VE GOT ROOM FOR HIM AS WELL.
TAKE HER TO CELL BLOCK NINE.
SHE'S NOT LYING ABOUT HER CONNECTION TO VADER. THE EMPIRE WILL BE SCOURING THE GALAXY FOR HER.
EVEN IF THEY COULD FIND US, WHICH THEY CAN'T, WE'RE QUITE WELL-DEFENDED HERE, PRINCESS. WE'VE GOT A STAR AT OUR BACK AND A SEA OF ION CANNONS IN FRONT OF US.
BELIEVE ME, AS HARD AS IT IS TO BREAK OUT OF THIS PLACE...

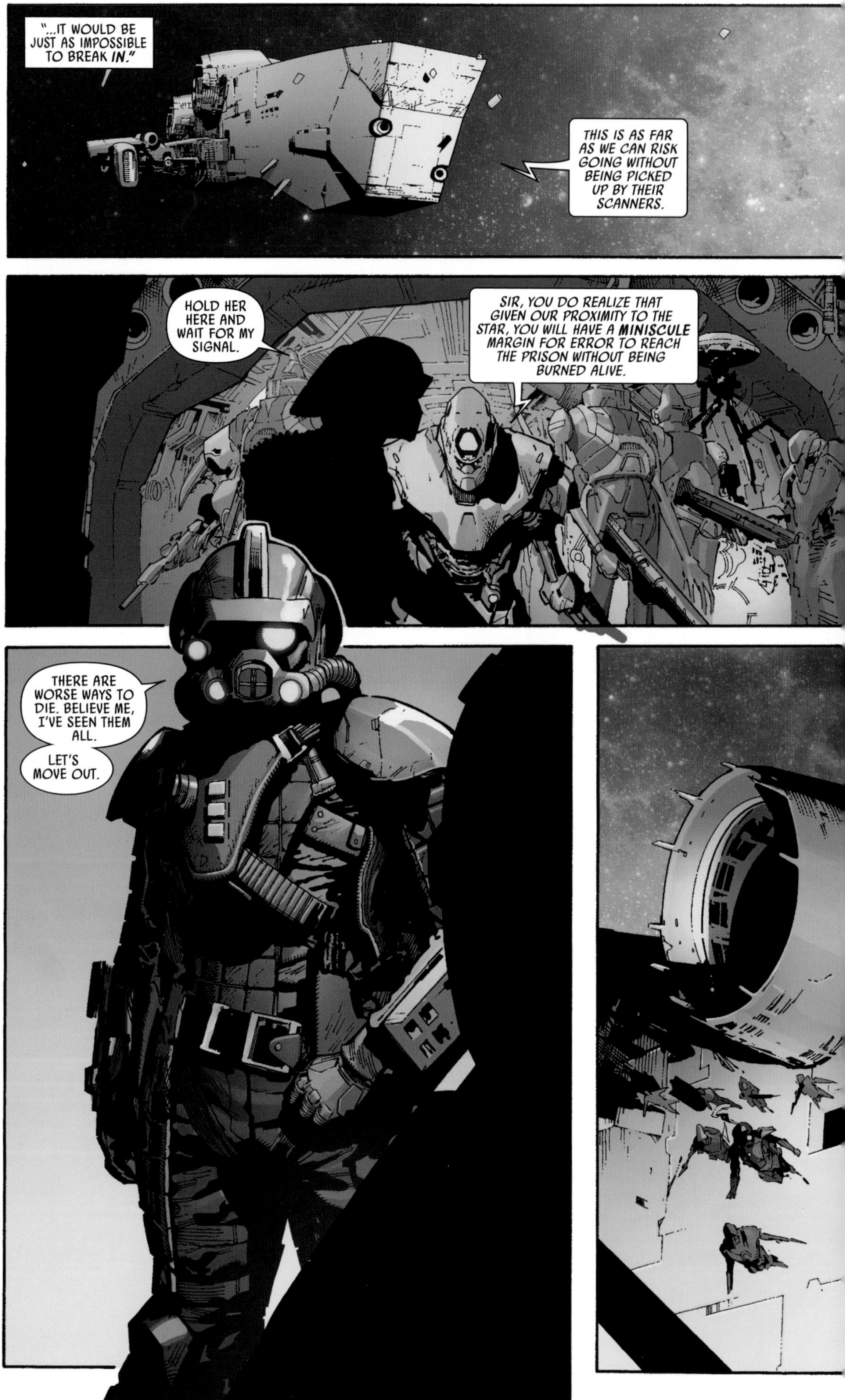
"...IT WOULD BE JUST AS IMPOSSIBLE TO BREAK IN."
THIS IS AS FAR AS WE CAN RISK GOING WITHOUT BEING PICKED UP BY THEIR SCANNERS.
HOLD HER HERE AND WAIT FOR MY SIGNAL.
SIR, YOU DO REALIZE THAT GIVEN OUR PROXIMITY TO THE STAR, YOU WILL HAVE A MINISCULE MARGIN FOR ERROR TO REACH THE PRISON WITHOUT BEING BURNED ALIVE.
THERE ARE WORSE WAYS TO DIE. BELIEVE ME, I'VE SEEN THEM ALL.
LET'S MOVE OUT.

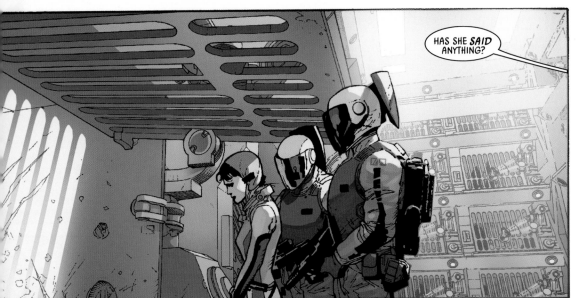

HAS SHE *SAID* ANYTHING?

OTHER THAN ELABORATELY GRUESOME THREATS AND THE MOST COLORFUL INSULTS I'VE EVER HEARD? NO.

SHE WAS QUESTIONED FOR WEEKS BY ALLIANCE INTELLIGENCE OFFICERS. SHE GAVE THEM NOTHING.

HMPH.

I BET IT WAS QUITE THE INTERROGATION. WHAT'D THEY DO, SHINE A BRIGHT LIGHT IN HER FACE? PLAY THEIR MUSIC REAL LOUD?

THE EMPIRE WOULDN'T STOP THERE.

WHICH IS ONE OF THE REASONS WE'RE FIGHTING A WAR AGAINST THEM, SANA.

AND ONE OF THE REASONS YOU'RE GOING TO *LOSE.*

HUMANITY ISN'T THE SAME AS WEAKNESS.

WHEN YOUR LIFE IS ON THE LINE, IT IS.

I REFUSE TO ACCEPT THAT.

TELL THAT TO A STORMTROOPER NEXT TIME YOU SEE ONE, AND SEE IF HE REFUSES TO KILL YOU.

AH, IF YOU'LL EXCUSE ME, LADIES, I BELIEVE I'LL SEE TO OUR PRISONER.

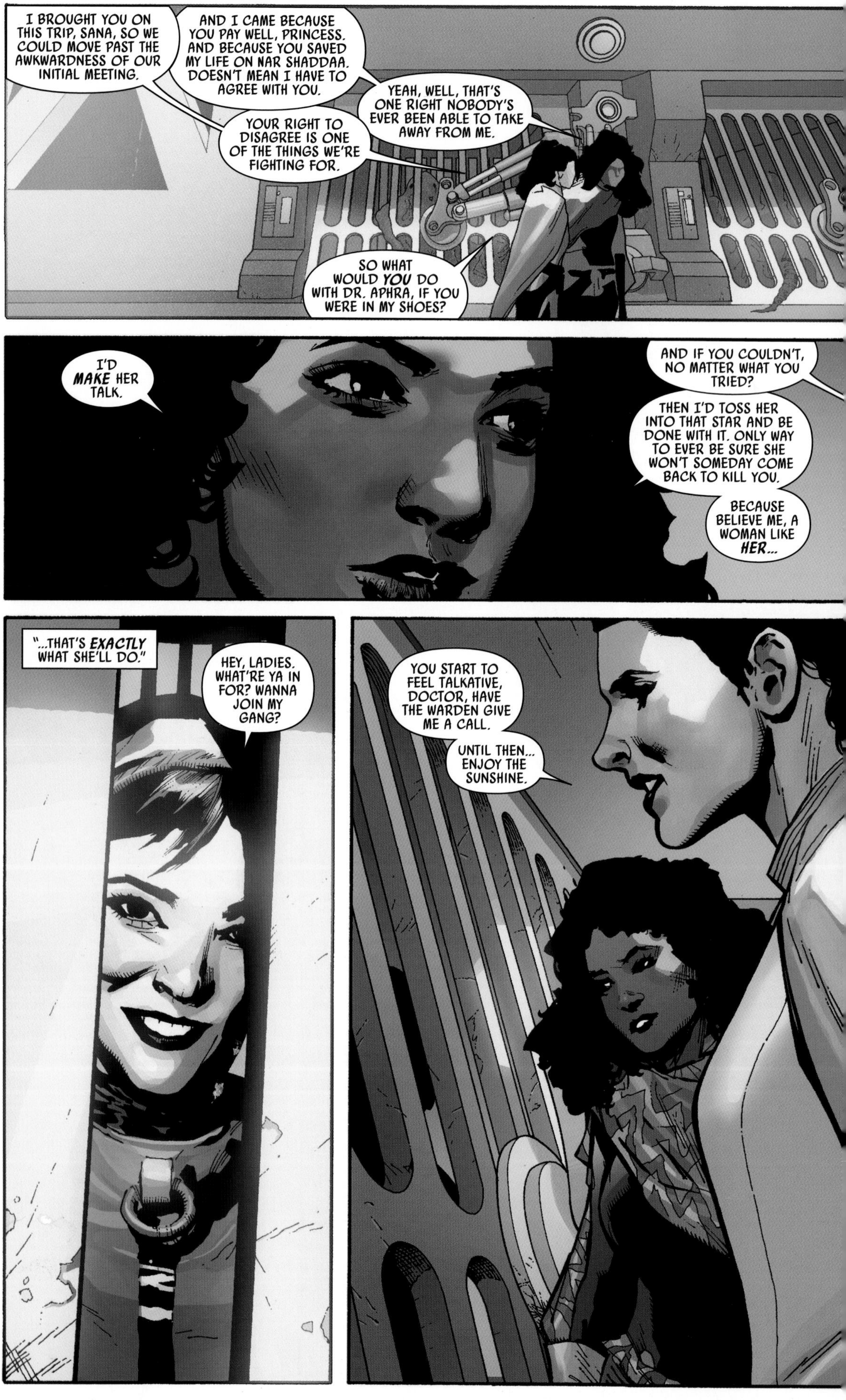
I BROUGHT YOU ON THIS TRIP, SANA, SO WE COULD MOVE PAST THE AWKWARDNESS OF OUR INITIAL MEETING.
AND I CAME BECAUSE YOU PAY WELL, PRINCESS. AND BECAUSE YOU SAVED MY LIFE ON NAR SHADDAA. DOESN'T MEAN I HAVE TO AGREE WITH YOU.
YOUR RIGHT TO DISAGREE IS ONE OF THE THINGS WE'RE FIGHTING FOR.
YEAH, WELL, THAT'S ONE RIGHT NOBODY'S EVER BEEN ABLE TO TAKE AWAY FROM ME.
SO WHAT WOULD YOU DO WITH DR. APHRA, IF YOU WERE IN MY SHOES?
I'D MAKE HER TALK.
AND IF YOU COULDN'T, NO MATTER WHAT YOU TRIED?
THEN I'D TOSS HER INTO THAT STAR AND BE DONE WITH IT. ONLY WAY TO EVER BE SURE SHE WON'T SOMEDAY COME BACK TO KILL YOU.
BECAUSE BELIEVE ME, A WOMAN LIKE HER...
"...THAT'S EXACTLY WHAT SHE'LL DO."
HEY, LADIES. WHAT'RE YA IN FOR? WANNA JOIN MY GANG?
YOU START TO FEEL TALKATIVE, DOCTOR, HAVE THE WARDEN GIVE ME A CALL.
UNTIL THEN... ENJOY THE SUNSHINE.

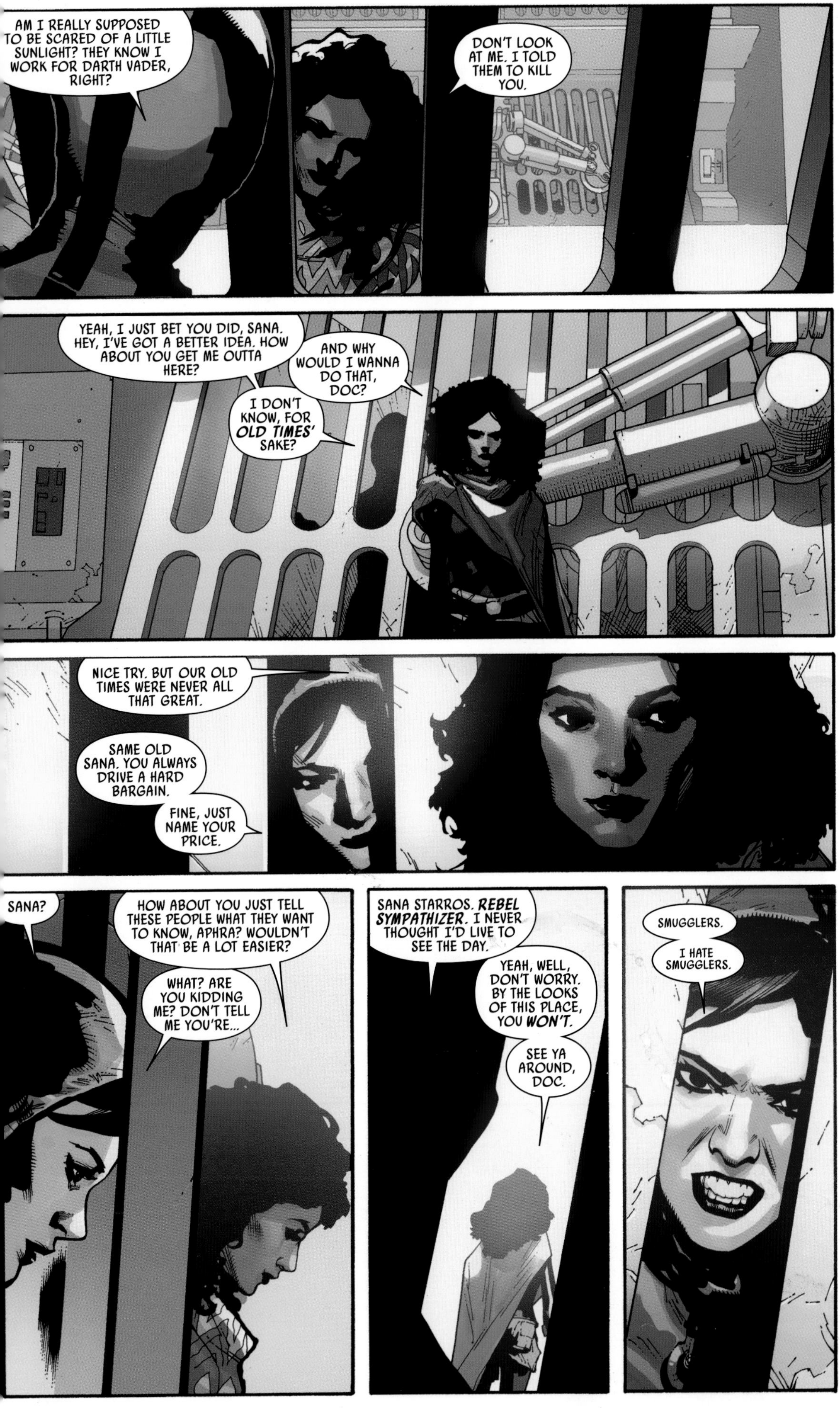
AM I REALLY SUPPOSED TO BE SCARED OF A LITTLE SUNLIGHT? THEY KNOW I WORK FOR DARTH VADER, RIGHT?
DON'T LOOK AT ME. I TOLD THEM TO KILL YOU.
YEAH, I JUST BET YOU DID, SANA. HEY, I'VE GOT A BETTER IDEA. HOW ABOUT YOU GET ME OUTTA HERE?
AND WHY WOULD I WANNA DO THAT, DOC?
I DON'T KNOW, FOR OLD TIMES' SAKE?
NICE TRY. BUT OUR OLD TIMES WERE NEVER ALL THAT GREAT.
SAME OLD SANA. YOU ALWAYS DRIVE A HARD BARGAIN.
FINE, JUST NAME YOUR PRICE.
SANA?
HOW ABOUT YOU JUST TELL THESE PEOPLE WHAT THEY WANT TO KNOW, APHRA? WOULDN'T THAT BE A LOT EASIER?
WHAT? ARE YOU KIDDING ME? DON'T TELL ME YOU'RE...
SANA STARROS. REBEL SYMPATHIZER. I NEVER THOUGHT I'D LIVE TO SEE THE DAY.
YEAH, WELL, DON'T WORRY. BY THE LOOKS OF THIS PLACE, YOU WON'T.
SEE YA AROUND, DOC.
SMUGGLERS.
I HATE SMUGGLERS.

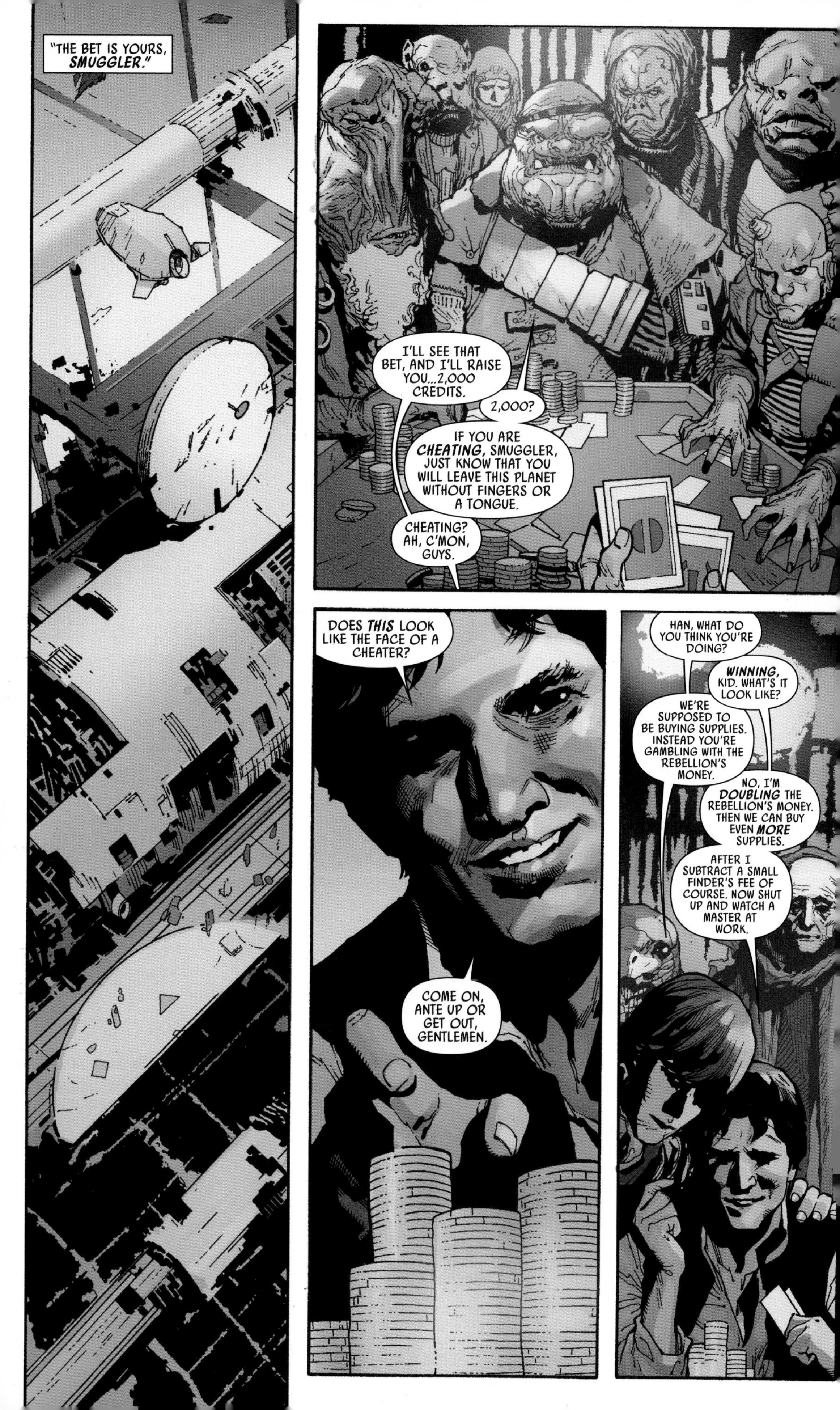
"THE BET IS YOURS, SMUGGLER."
I'LL SEE THAT BET, AND I'LL RAISE YOU...2,000 CREDITS.
2,000?
IF YOU ARE CHEATING, SMUGGLER, JUST KNOW THAT YOU WILL LEAVE THIS PLANET WITHOUT FINGERS OR A TONGUE.
CHEATING? AH, C'MON, GUYS.
DOES THIS LOOK LIKE THE FACE OF A CHEATER?
COME ON, ANTE UP OR GET OUT, GENTLEMEN.
HAN, WHAT DO YOU THINK YOU'RE DOING?
WINNING, KID. WHAT'S IT LOOK LIKE?
WE'RE SUPPOSED TO BE BUYING SUPPLIES. INSTEAD YOU'RE GAMBLING WITH THE REBELLION'S MONEY.
NO, I'M DOUBLING THE REBELLION'S MONEY. THEN WE CAN BUY EVEN MORE SUPPLIES.
AFTER I SUBTRACT A SMALL FINDER'S FEE OF COURSE. NOW SHUT UP AND WATCH A MASTER AT WORK.

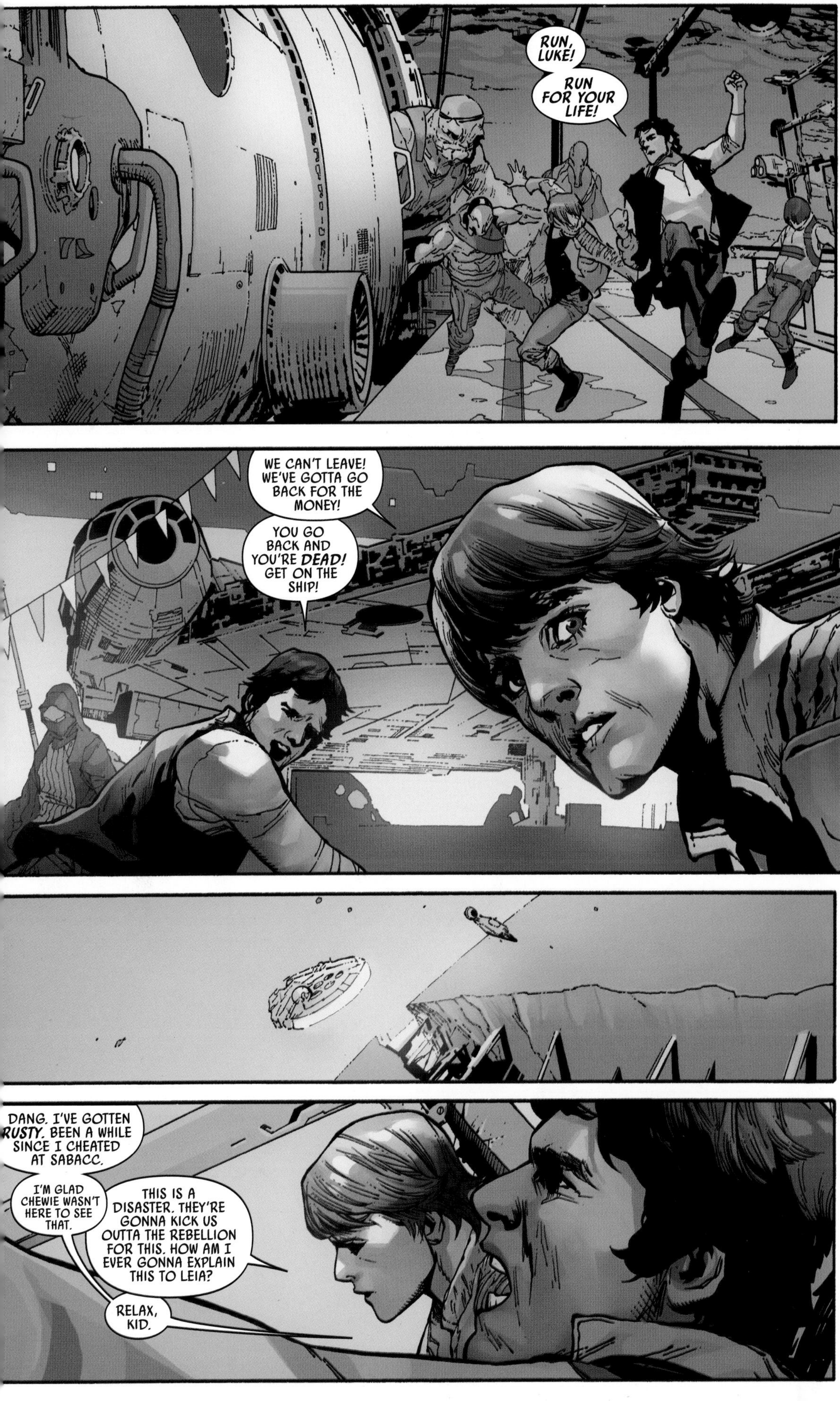
RUN, LUKE!
RUN FOR YOUR LIFE!
WE CAN'T LEAVE! WE'VE GOTTA GO BACK FOR THE MONEY!
YOU GO BACK AND YOU'RE DEAD! GET ON THE SHIP!
DANG. I'VE GOTTEN RUSTY. BEEN A WHILE SINCE I CHEATED AT SABACC.
I'M GLAD CHEWIE WASN'T HERE TO SEE THAT.
THIS IS A DISASTER. THEY'RE GONNA KICK US OUTTA THE REBELLION FOR THIS. HOW AM I EVER GONNA EXPLAIN THIS TO LEIA?
RELAX, KID.

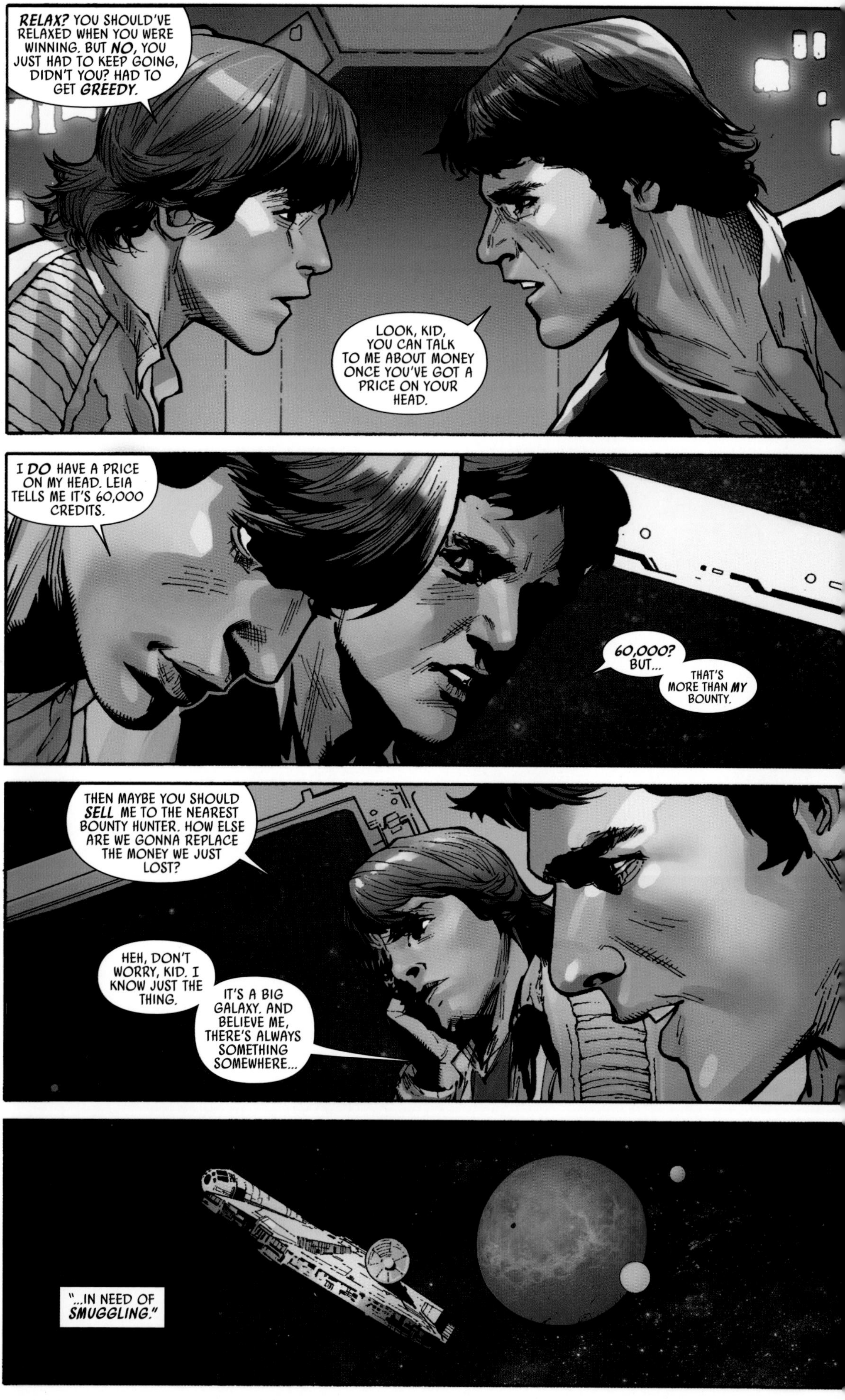

RELAX? YOU SHOULD'VE RELAXED WHEN YOU WERE WINNING. BUT NO, YOU JUST HAD TO KEEP GOING, DIDN'T YOU? HAD TO GET GREEDY.
LOOK, KID, YOU CAN TALK TO ME ABOUT MONEY ONCE YOU'VE GOT A PRICE ON YOUR HEAD.
I DO HAVE A PRICE ON MY HEAD. LEIA TELLS ME IT'S 60,000 CREDITS.
60,000? BUT...
THAT'S MORE THAN MY BOUNTY.
THEN MAYBE YOU SHOULD SELL ME TO THE NEAREST BOUNTY HUNTER. HOW ELSE ARE WE GONNA REPLACE THE MONEY WE JUST LOST?
HEH, DON'T WORRY, KID. I KNOW JUST THE THING.
IT'S A BIG GALAXY. AND BELIEVE ME, THERE'S ALWAYS SOMETHING SOMEWHERE...
"...IN NEED OF SMUGGLING."

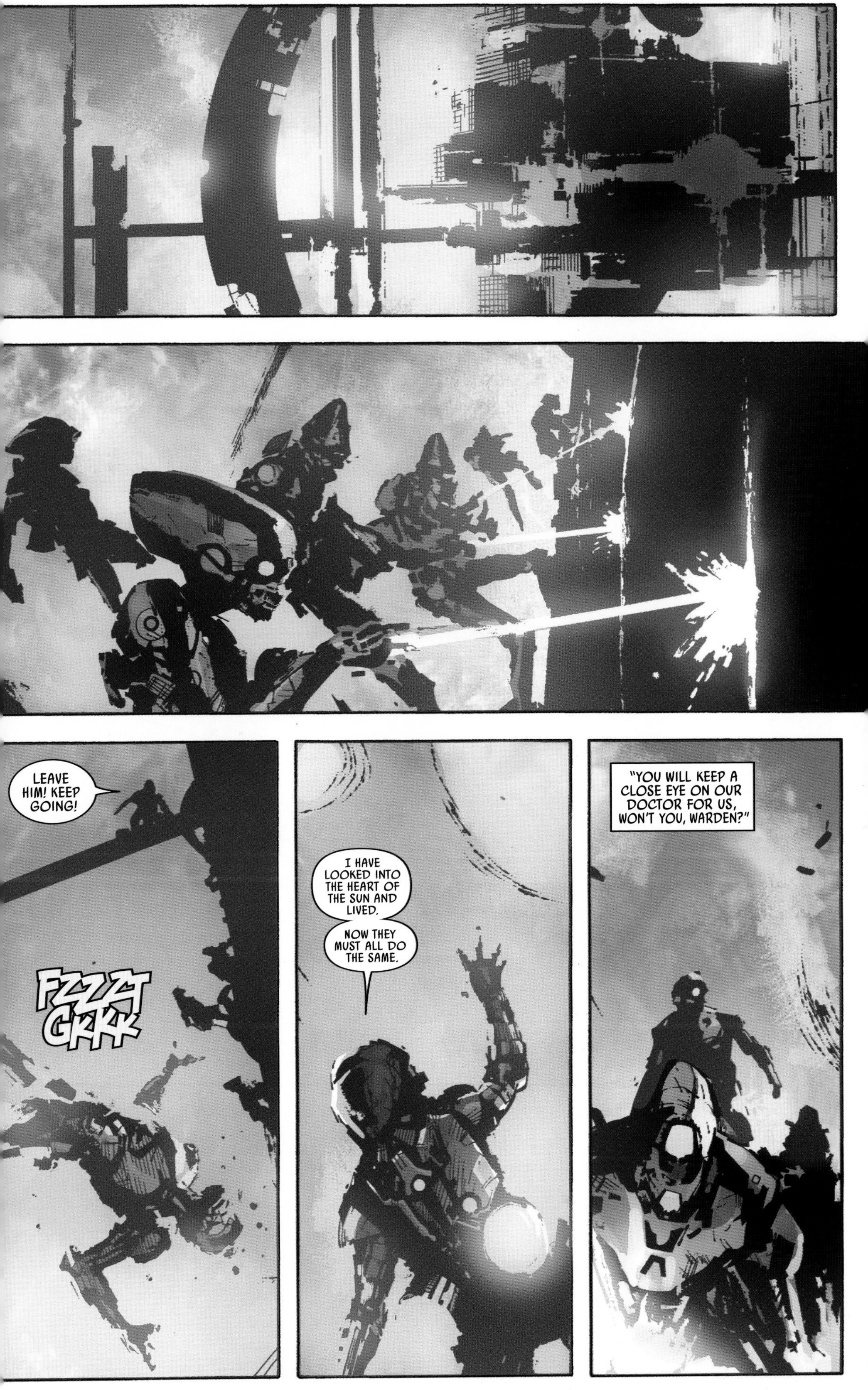
LEAVE HIM! KEEP GOING!
FZZZT GKKK
I HAVE LOOKED INTO THE HEART OF THE SUN AND LIVED.
NOW THEY MUST ALL DO THE SAME.
"YOU WILL KEEP A CLOSE EYE ON OUR DOCTOR FOR US, WON'T YOU, WARDEN?"

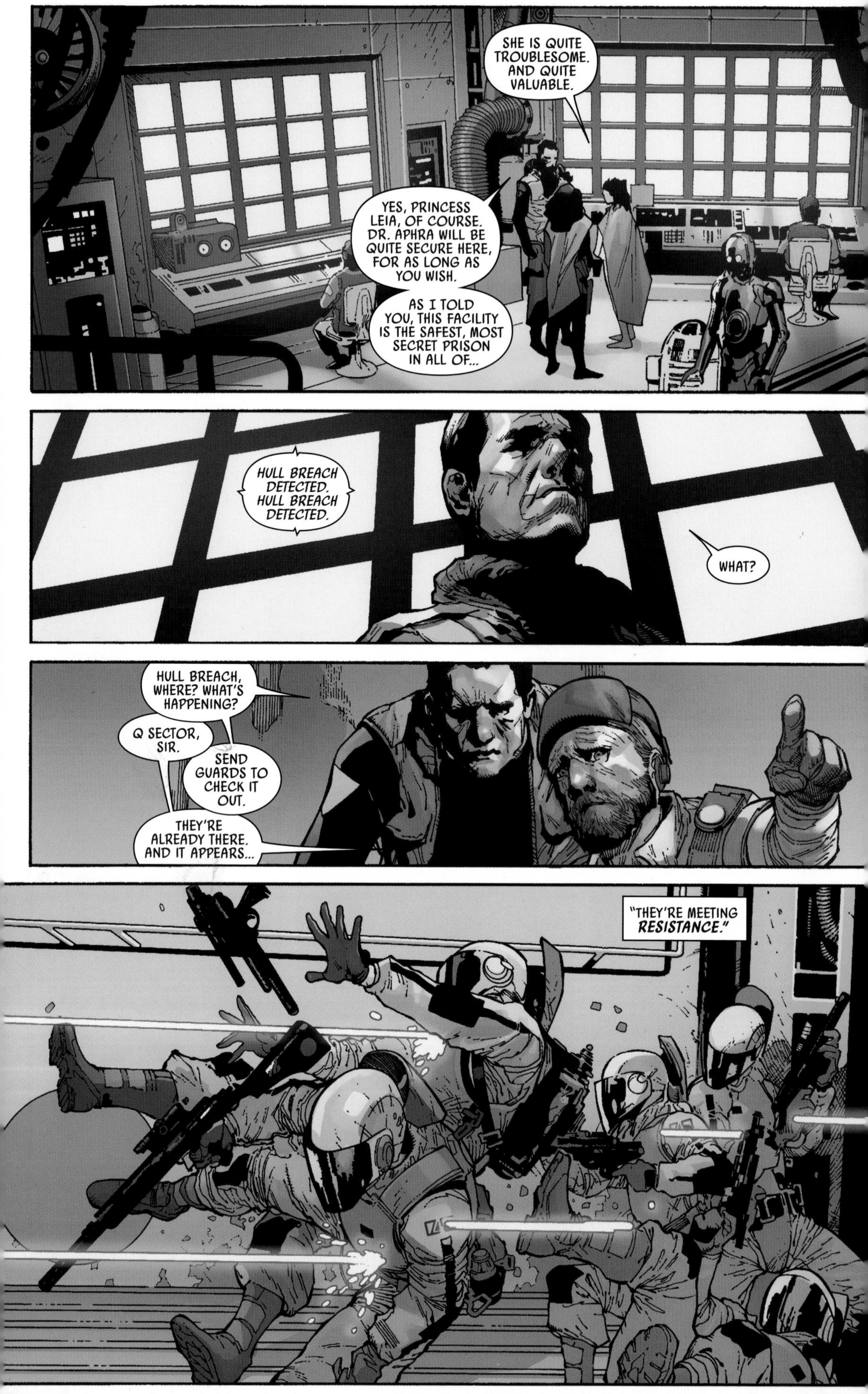
SHE IS QUITE TROUBLESOME. AND QUITE VALUABLE.
YES, PRINCESS LEIA, OF COURSE. DR. APHRA WILL BE QUITE SECURE HERE, FOR AS LONG AS YOU WISH.
AS I TOLD YOU, THIS FACILITY IS THE SAFEST, MOST SECRET PRISON IN ALL OF...
HULL BREACH DETECTED. HULL BREACH DETECTED.
WHAT?
HULL BREACH, WHERE? WHAT'S HAPPENING?
Q SECTOR, SIR.
SEND GUARDS TO CHECK IT OUT.
THEY'RE ALREADY THERE. AND IT APPEARS...
"THEY'RE MEETING RESISTANCE."

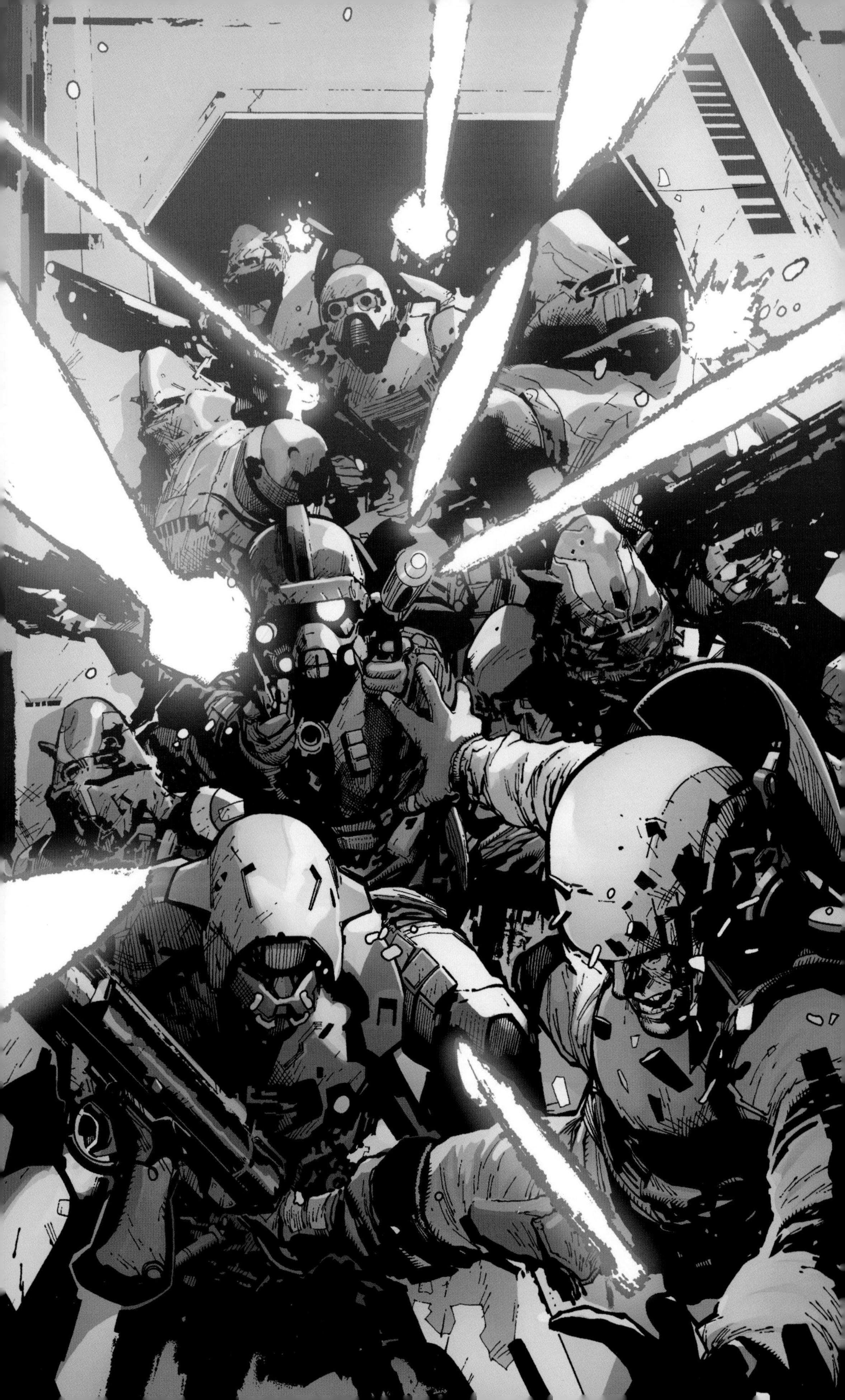

STAR WARS™

REBEL JAIL

COLLECT THEM ALL!

Set of 5 Hardcover Books ISBN: 978-1-5321-4140-9

STAR WARS
STAR WARS
REBEL JAIL: VOLUME 1
AARON MAYHEW

Hardcover Book ISBN
978-1-5321-4141-6

STAR WARS
STAR WARS
REBEL JAIL: VOLUME 2
AARON YU ALANGUILAN GHO

Hardcover Book ISBN
978-1-5321-4142-3

STAR WARS
STAR WARS
REBEL JAIL: VOLUME 3
AARON YU GHO

Hardcover Book ISBN
978-1-5321-4143-0

STAR WARS
STAR WARS
REBEL JAIL: VOLUME 4
AARON YU ALANGUILAN GHO

Hardcover Book ISBN

STAR WARS
STAR WARS
REBEL JAIL: VOLUME 5
AARON YU ALANGUILAN GHO TARTAGLIA

Hardcover Book ISBN

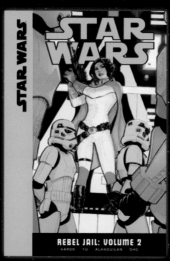

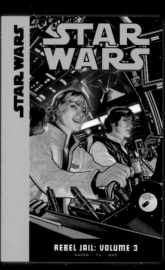

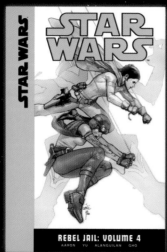